JUL   2020

HOORAY FOR
LOLO

Written and Illustrated
by Niki Daly

To Nadia Ismail
Champion Librarian
Love—Niki

Xhosa words in *Hurray for Lolo*
Molo: hello
Yebo: yes

––––––––––––––––––––––––––––––––

Catalyst Press
Pacifica, California

For further information,
write Catalyst Press, info@catalystpress.org.

Originally published in 2019 by Otter-Barry Books in Great Britain

FIRST EDITION 10 9 8 7 6 5 4 3 2 1

Library of Congress Control Number: 2019951217

Illustrated with digital art

Set in Maiandra GD

.

HOORAY FOR
LOLO

Written and Illustrated by Niki Daly

CATALYST
PRESS

Contents

Lolo's Worst Best Friend

"That Lulu Dlamini is such a show-off!"
said Lolo. "She always has to be better than
everyone else!"

"What do you mean?" asked Mama.
"I thought Lulu was your best friend."

"Not when she's showing off," said Lolo.
"Then she's my worst best friend."

"What's she got to show off about?"
asked Gogo.

"Like today in class," said Lolo, "she told everyone that she was getting a fancy phone for her birthday."

"Her parents must be very rich to afford such an expensive birthday present," said Mama.

"She says her mother's a fashion model, her father owns a candy factory, and they all live in a mansion with a swimming pool," said Lolo. "It's not fair!"

"Being rich can't buy happiness,"
said Gogo.

"Well, Lulu is very rich and is *always*
happy!" said Lolo.

The next day was Wear-Your-Own-Clothes Day. Mama made sure that Lolo's favorite T-shirt was washed and ironed. It went nicely with her polka-dot skirt and stripy tights.

"You look like a
cool cat," said Gogo.
Lolo smiled. She
felt cool.

And her favorite blue sneakers made
her feel like bouncing to school.

9

But when Lolo skipped into the
playground, all the bounce went out of
her step. Lulu was surrounded by a group
of girls... and she was showing off!

"My father bought my *I love New York* T-shirt in New York," said Lulu.

"That's in Johannesburg," said Dana Rose.

"No, it's not, Stupid!" snapped Lulu. "It's in America."

That's another thing Lolo didn't like about Lulu. If you didn't know something, she always called you *stupid.*

Later, during break, Lulu started handing out party invitations to all the girls.

"It's going to be a girls' sleepover party," she said. "There'll be a party bag for everyone and extra-large pizzas, and the biggest heart-shaped cake you've *ever* seen!"

All the Year 3 girls

got an invitation.

All except Lolo.

It made her want to cry. She pinched her eyes so that the tears would stay inside her. But when she got home, she burst into tears.

Gogo tried to make her feel better by saying, "Who wants to go to Little Miss Show-Off's birthday, anyway?" But that made not being invited even worse.

It was horrid being left out when the rest of the girls in her class had been invited.

"Maybe you can have your own sleepover and invite friends who are nice to you," said Gogo.

"Maybe, if you're nice to Lulu, she'll invite you to her party," said Mama.

Lolo thought about it and thought about it. And the more she thought about it, the more she decided she would just be *herself* and see what might happen.

So, the next day when she arrived

at school, Lolo was "Lolo."

And this is what happened....

As she walked into the classroom,
someone tapped her on her shoulder. And
when she turned round, Lulu handed her
an invitation.

"I ran out of them yesterday," she
explained. "So I made you a special one with
my special glitter pens from Hong Kong."

And what a special card it was.

Something to *really* show off!

The party was special, too. BUT...

Lulu did NOT live in a mansion with a swimming pool.

She lived in a very nice house with a porta-pool.

And the party bags turned out to be
surprise packets made by Lulu's dad, who
worked in a supermarket. And...

Lulu's mom was not a fashion model.
She was a hairdresser, and she kept telling
Lulu not to show off in front of her friends.

They DID

have pizzas—

small ones.

There WAS a birthday cake
in the shape of a heart.

But it
wasn't
THAT
big.

Lulu did NOT get a fancy phone for her birthday. Still, Lulu looked happy!

And Lolo was *very* happy that her worst best friend was happy and had stopped showing off at last!

Lolo's First Library Book

Lolo walked into the library with Gogo. She liked the smell of the new building. She liked the shelves of books and shiny tables.

Today she hoped to find something special to read, a storybook—with pictures!

She held Gogo's warm hand as they walked into the room where all the children's books were kept. A lady at a desk looked up and smiled. She wore a little badge. On it was written *LIBRARIAN*.

"Lolo would like to borrow a book from the library," said Gogo.

"Lovely!" said the librarian and
handed Gogo a form to fill out.

Lolo walked around the room slowly. Some books were on shelves too high for her to reach. Some books she could reach, but they had too many words and no pictures.

Gogo sat down on a little yellow chair at a little green table and started to fill in the form.

"I like it here," whispered Lolo.

Gogo looked up and smiled.

"Why don't you find a nice book to take home?" asked Gogo.

"Let me show you where the picture books are kept, Lolo," said the nice librarian, whose name was Nadia.

Lolo followed Nadia to shelves that were just the right height for her.

"Take your time," said Nadia. "I'm sure you'll find just the right book for you."

By the time Gogo handed in the form, Lolo had found just the right book— a book about a terrible monster with horns and tusks.

"This looks very scary," said Gogo. "Let's see if there's one that won't give you nightmares."

"*This* looks like a lovely book," said Gogo, showing Lolo a book that had a fairy in a pink ballet dress.

But Lolo knew what she liked and she knew what she wanted.

So she held on to her book tightly.

"Ah, everyone likes this book," said Nadia.

Lolo looked carefully as her book was stamped with the date that she would have to return it.

"There you go!" said Nadia, handing Lolo her first library book and her first library card.

Lolo was so happy!

"Carry it nicely," said Gogo. And they left.

That book! What a story! What pictures! Even Gogo said it was the best children's story she had ever read.

So the following Friday, Lolo took the library book to school for Mrs. Rhode, her teacher, to read and show the pictures.

The children laughed and loved the story. Especially Themba, who wanted it to be read again and again. But Mrs. Rhode closed it and gave it to Lolo to put back safely in her bag.

That evening at bedtime, Gogo said, "Lolo, tomorrow we must take your book back to the library. So, tonight we must read that funny story one last time."

Lolo opened her bag, but the library book was not there!

"Oh, Lolo," said Gogo, "you must have left it at school!"

"No," said Lolo, "I put it in my bag when Mrs. Rhode gave it back to me!"

She wanted to cry.

What would the librarian say?

"Who would take it from your bag?" asked Gogo.

Lolo thought and thought.

"Themba Nombela!" cried Lolo. "He
loved the story so much, he wanted it to be
read again and again!"

"Does Themba steal?" asked Gogo.

"Themba sometimes takes things without
asking. But he always brings them back."

The next morning, Gogo and Lolo went to the Nombelas' house to see if Themba had the library book.

"Yes," said Themba. "I meant to bring it back, but Zinzi Dube borrowed it from me."

So Themba showed Gogo and Lolo where the Dubes lived.

"Tata has it," said Zinzi.
"He can't read, but he
wanted to look at
the pictures."

So off went Zinzi,
Themba, Lolo and Gogo to Tata's house,
where they found him sitting outside his
front door laughing his head off.

"Ha, ha, ha! Zinzi, this book is too, too funny! I am enjoying it very much," said the old man.

Gogo explained that the book belonged to the library and they only had a few minutes to get it back on time.

Lolo had never seen Gogo walk so fast. But when they reached the library, the door was closed.

Gogo read the notice and said, "It will only open again on Monday."

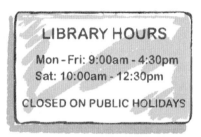

LIBRARY HOURS
Mon - Fri: 9:00am - 4:30pm
Sat: 10:00am - 12:30pm

CLOSED ON PUBLIC HOLIDAYS

"But Gogo, the librarian will be very cross."

"Don't worry about that," said Gogo, "I will explain what happened. I am sure she will understand what can happen when a book is as nice as this one. Everyone wants to read it! And until Monday, we can enjoy it a bit more."

When Monday afternoon came, Gogo and Lolo took the book to the library.

Nadia noticed that it was late. But when Gogo explained why, Nadia smiled and said, "That's a wonderful story! Lolo, next time, bring your friends to join the library...and Grandfather too. We teach people to read on Friday mornings."

And that's exactly what happened.

Thabo, Zinzi, and lots of Lolo's school friends have joined the library.

Even Zinzi's grandfather has joined!

He likes the new words he learns to read every Friday.

But the books he likes most of all are the ones with pictures that make him laugh!

What Made Lolo Smile

Lolo woke up with a tummy ache.

"Stay in bed today, Lolo," said Mama.

"Perhaps you'll feel better tomorrow and

then you can go to school."

But the next day, Lolo felt worse. Her
tummy ached, her head ached, and she'd
lost her smile.

"Poor Lolo," said Mama. "We'll have to
go to the clinic." Mama helped Lolo get
dressed while Gogo went outside to wave
down a taxi.

"Emergency!" cried Gogo as the taxi screeched to a halt. "My grandchild is very sick and needs to go to the clinic," she explained to the taxi driver.

"No problem!" said the taxi driver.

As soon as Mama and Lolo climbed into the taxi, off they sped.

Poor Lolo felt as though she was going to be sick as the taxi bumped and zigzagged through the traffic. She rested her head against Mama's soft body.

A lady smiled at Lolo, but Lolo just closed her eyes. Lolo had lost her smile.

"Paarp!" went the taxi, jerking to a stop outside the clinic.

A nurse took Lolo's temperature, then immediately called the doctor.

Mama helped Lolo undress so that the doctor could examine her.

"This won't hurt," said the nice doctor. But Lolo went "ouch!" when the doctor pressed gently against her tummy. The doctor explained what was wrong with Lolo.

It was

APPENDICITIS,

and Lolo had to go immediately to
the big hospital.

"Go quickly!" said the doctor. "Our
ambulance is leaving for the hospital
right now."

52

The ambulance drove even faster than the taxi.

"Wheeoow! Wheeoow! Wheeoow!"

Oh dear! Just before they arrived, Lolo was sick into a bag. Afterwards she felt a little better. But still—no smiles.

As soon as they reached the hospital, Mama lifted Lolo in her arms and ran through the entrance, straight into the waiting room.

Mama and Lolo waited and waited until their names were called: "Mrs. Twala and Lolo!"

They followed the young doctor down one passage, into an elevator and out again, then down another passage with Lolo's sneakers going squeak, squeak on the shiny floor. At last they stopped at a door with a sign that read:

"MRI"

"This won't take long," said the doctor, "and then we'll know what will make Lolo feel better."

The doctor helped Lolo lie on a bed that went slowly through a tunnel. It made a sound like Mama's washing machine.

And there, on a screen, they saw a strange picture. *It was what Lolo looked like inside!*

"This is Lolo's appendix," said the doctor, pointing to a small white blob. "See, it's swollen. That's why Lolo feels so sick."

"What are you going to do?" asked Mama.

"We'll remove it tomorrow," said the doctor.

"Don't worry, Lolo. You will be asleep for a while, and when you wake up it will all be over."

She gave Lolo a big smile, but Lolo did not have one to give her.

The next morning, Lolo was wheeled into the operating room. The surgeon winked at her through his green mask and told her to count to ten.

One, two, three, four, five, six, seven, eight, nine… and then Lolo was asleep.

Lolo slept while the clever surgeon cut a tiny slit in her tummy and removed her appendix. Soon it was OUT. Then the doctor closed the tiny slit with stitches—and it was ALL OVER!

When Lolo finally woke up, Mama and Gogo were there. "How are you feeling, Lolo?" they asked.

"It feels like someone is pinching my tummy," said Lolo. Gogo gave her toes a little tickle. But *that* did not bring back Lolo's smile.

And when Mama told her that she had to stay one more day and one more night in hospital, *that* made Lolo frown!

During the day a very
important doctor came
to see Lolo. He had
a funny mustache.
But it did not make Lolo smile.

Next, a lady asked Lolo
how to spell her surname.
She wore funny spectacles.
But they did not make
Lolo smile.

Then a man with a silly hat
read a funny story.

All the children laughed
and laughed, except Lolo.

Later, a nurse brought Lolo a
bowl of wobbly jello. But that
didn't make Lolo smile. All
Lolo wanted was to go home.
But then...

that evening, Evalina, the cleaning lady, came down the passage. And when she looked into the ward, she knew at once what a little girl with a frown needed.

So Evalina started to sing and dance, this way and that way, with her mop.

63

Evalina reminded Lolo of Gogo. And her mop, with its flying braids, reminded her of Mama. *Yebo!* Her mama and Gogo were coming to take her home tomorrow!

And *that's* what made Lolo smile!

Lolo the Babysitter

It was a Saturday morning when baby Bongi arrived.

"Aunty Albertina has to be at the morning market to sell her necklaces, so I've offered to babysit," Mama explained to Lolo.

"Lolo can help," said Gogo.

"Why can't Aunty Albertina take her baby with her?" asked Lolo, who had plans of her own.

"Because if he cries, I can't see to my customers," explained Aunty Albertina.

"It will be fun to have a baby in the house," said Mama.

"But babies cry all the time," said Lolo.

"Oh, I remember when *you* were a baby," said Gogo. "It was *waa*, *waa*, *waa* all the time!"

And the minute Aunty Albertina left, that's exactly what baby Bongi did.

"*WAA! WAA! WAA!*"

WAA! WAA! WAA!

"Lolo, please rock the baby buggy. Babies like being rocked," said Gogo.

So Lolo rocked the baby buggy.

"Not so hard…" said Gogo, "…gently."

Lolo did it gently, and baby Bongi stopped crying.

"There," whispered Gogo.

"He's falling asleep."

"Breakfast is ready," called Mama.

On tippy-toes, Lolo and Gogo followed the yummy smell of eggs and bacon into the kitchen.

"So what are your plans for this morning?" Mama asked Lolo.

"I'm going to wash Nichelle's ball gown," said Lolo. Then she thought some more. "And string beads...and...and..."

"What busy mornings you are both going to have," said Gogo. "I'm going to put my feet up and see what's on TV."

"I'm going to do some housework and then we can all go to the shopping mall when Albertina picks up baby Bongi," said Mama.

But just then, they stopped doing what they were all doing because...

"WAA! WAA! WAA!" went baby Bongi.

WAA! WAA! WAA!

"I'll go and
see to him,"
said Mama.

"He needs his diaper changed," said
Mama, coming back with baby Bongi.

"*Poo!*" said Lolo.

"Come and help me, Lolo," said Mama.

"*No way!*" said Lolo, holding her nose.

"Go on," said Gogo. "One day you'll
have your own baby and then you'll know
how to change a diaper."

Lolo followed Mama and the
smelly baby into the lounge.

Mama laid baby Bongi down on a towel.

Then she removed his smelly diaper and dropped it into a plastic carrier bag.

She sent Lolo off to fill a bowl with warm water to wipe baby Bongi's bottom clean.

"Powder please,"
said Mama.
And Lolo handed her
the baby powder.

"Clean diaper please," said Mama.

And Lolo handed her
a clean diaper.

"There!" said
Mama. "Powder
bottom! Now he's
happy!"

Mama picked up baby Bongi and looked at Lolo.

"Would you like to hold him?" asked Mama.

"No way," said Lolo, *"*I've got lots to do."

First, Lolo did her washing. Then she hung Nichelle's ball gown on the line.

Next, she opened her box of beads,
but before she could string one...

"WAA! WAA! WAA!"

WAA! WAA! WAA!

Mama said, "Lolo, will you *pleeease* help me? Baby Bongi needs a song."

So Gogo switched off the TV. And Mama showed Lolo how to hold baby Bongi safely on her lap.

"Let's sing *Lala 'baba'* to him," said Gogo.

"Lala 'baba' lala!

Go to sleep baby boy!"

After a while, Mama took sleepy baby Bongi from Lolo and settled him back in his buggy.

Gogo went on watching TV. And Lolo
went to check if Nichelle's dress was drying
on the line. It was dry, so she dressed
Nichelle.

"WAA! WAA! WAA!"

This time baby Bongi was hungry.

So Mama fed him and sat him on the floor with some puffy pillows.

"Lolo," asked Mama, "will you please play with baby Bongi? I have so many things still to do."

Well, Lolo also had lots of things to do, but she also liked to help Mama, so…

She clapped hands with baby Bongi.

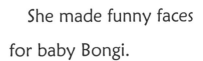

She made funny faces for baby Bongi.

She sang all her school
songs for baby Bongi.

She tickled baby Bongi.

She even let baby
Bongi hold Nichelle.

And whenever he went *"WAA! WAA! WAA!"* Lolo did something to make him blow bubbles and giggle.

By the time Aunty Albertina returned,
Lolo was very, very tired from playing
with baby Bongi.

"Here's a 'thank you' present for being such a good babysitter," said Aunty Albertina, as she tied one of her beautiful beaded necklaces round Lolo's neck.

"Thank you," said Lolo, with a BIG yawn.

Mama looked at Gogo and said, "Oh dear, Lolo is too tired to come shopping with us today."

Yebo! Lolo's eyes had started to close.

Gogo giggled. "*Eish!* It looks as though the babysitter needs a babysitter," she joked.

So Gogo stayed at home...

while Lolo slept…

and slept…

and slept.

Niki Daly

has won many awards for his work.
His groundbreaking *Not So Fast Songololo*, winner
of a US Parent's Choice Award, paved the way
for post-apartheid South African children's books.
Among his many books, *Once Upon a Time* was
an Honor Winner in the US Children's Africana Book
Awards and *Jamela's Dress* was chosen by the
ALA as a Notable Children's Book and by Booklist
as one of the Top 10 African American Picture Books—
it also won both the Children's Literature
Choice Award and the Parents' Choice Silver Award.
Niki wrote and illustrated the picture book
Surprise! Surprise! for Otter-Barry Books.
He lives with his wife, the author and illustrator
Jude Daly, in South Africa.

Also available in the Lolo series